The Lighthouse Dog

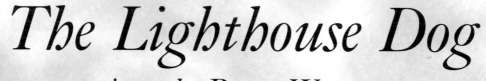

The Lighthouse Dog

written by Betty Waterton
illustrations by Dean Griffiths

ORCA BOOK PUBLISHERS

ONE day the captain's wife put her town hat on her head, her town shoes on her feet and her shopping bag over her arm.

"Today is market day in town, and I'm going to get a puppy," she told her husband. "My friend Flossie is going to help me choose it, and oh, I can hardly wait!"

"Well, if you must, you must," sighed the captain. "But just get a small one."

"I will," said his wife.

As she climbed into her little rowboat, he said, "And don't forget to bring home a pizza for supper. A large one!"

"I won't," promised his wife. And with the oars in the oarlocks gently squeaking, she rowed away from the lighthouse.

As she neared town, the captain's wife saw someone with frizzy hair jumping up and down on the dock. It was her friend Flossie.

"Hurry, hurry!" shouted Flossie. "Or they'll all be gone!"

But when they got to the market, they found there were still lots of puppies left. Black ones, brown ones, yellow and white — some with spots and some with splotches. And one really BIG dark one.

"I can't choose," cried the captain's wife. "I love them all! But I especially love that really big practically black one with the pink necktie."

"That's not a necktie, that's her tongue," said Flossie. "She's almost a real Newfie. I think."

"I do love her the most, but she's SO BIG …"

"She just seems big," said Flossie. "You could name her 'Molly,' after my grandmother on my mother's side."

"I love that name," said the captain's wife.

So the captain's wife bought the big dog and named her Molly. She bought a big bag of dog crumbles and some jumbo milk bones. Then she and Flossie had a nice fish-and-chips lunch.

"Don't forget the pizza," said Flossie. "Get one with olives."

So the captain's wife bought a Super-Duper-Special-De-Luxe salami pizza with olives to take home to the captain. Then they all went back to the boat.

"Thanks for all your help, Flossie," shouted the captain's wife, as she rowed away. But her friend Flossie had already gone — back home to help her mother make beeswax candles.

Meanwhile, the captain had finished doing all his lighthouse things. He had made himself a bowl of almost-instant seaweed soup for lunch, and now he was dozing on the beach, dreaming of pizzas.

He woke up when he heard the splashing of oars in the water. There was his wife, rowing wearily towards him, her hat all askew. And there was someone in a practically black fur coat. A fur coat?!!

Suddenly there was a gigantic splash as Molly jumped out of the boat and into the water. She swam to shore, shook herself and lumbered over to the captain. Putting her front paws on his shoulders, she mopped his face lovingly with her big, pink tongue. The captain toppled over backwards.

"This is Molly, our new puppy," said his wife, as she helped him up. "Flossie says she's almost a real Newfoundland."

"That's a puppy?" cried the captain, wiping his face with his handkerchief.

"Sort of an old puppy, I guess. Flossie says she just seems big. Now, come into the house and see what I brought you."

Smacking his lips, the captain peered into the shopping bag. But all that was left of the Super-Duper-Special-De-Luxe salami pizza were some crumbs and five olives.

"Oh, dear," said the captain's wife. "Well, at least now we know Molly doesn't like olives. But not to worry, I'll make you some almost-instant seaweed soup."

"I'm getting mighty tired of that," grumbled the captain.

Molly ate two dishpans full of dog crumbles. Then she took Corky the cat off the chesterfield and placed him on top of the piano. After that, she stretched out on the chesterfield herself, and went to sleep.

The next day Molly carried Corky the cat outside and put him, yowling, into the little rowboat. She towed it around to the far side of the island and hid the oars in the bushes. She dumped Corky's cat crumbles into the sea. She ate the hat of the captain's wife, and buried her town shoes under some kelp.

"She's just feeling insecure," said the captain's wife. "She's afraid she's going to be sent back to town."

When they found sixteen starfish and a baby crab in their bed, the captain merely grunted. And when he found his favourite furry slippers all sticky around the edges, he groaned. But when Molly ate their whole Thanksgiving dinner — including the pumpkin pie — he cried, "That's it. Enough!"

His wife sighed and blew her nose. "I guess Molly isn't working out too well, is she?"

"You might say that," said her husband. "I think you'd better take her back to the market tomorrow."

But the next morning when they looked outside, there were whitecaps on the water. "It's too rough today," said the captain.

The day after that the sea was an ominous dark green, and purple clouds scudded across the sky. "There's a storm coming," he told his wife. "You certainly can't go to town today."

On the third day the wind blew salt spray against the windows. The lighthouse beacon flashed and the big bell on the rocks clanged. "I hope there is nobody out there in this storm," said the captain.

But that very evening his wife suddenly cried out, "I think I hear somebody calling … "

The captain opened the door and listened. "So do I! There is somebody out there! I must rescue them!"

He took his lantern, and raced down to the dock. The waves were washing right over it.

From somewhere out on the water, a voice called: "HELP!"

"I'M COMING!" The captain jumped into his lifesaving boat and pulled the starter cord. Again and again he pulled it. But the motor would not start.

Just then Molly hurtled past him. She plunged into the crashing sea and began swimming. Then she was gone — into the black, stormy night.

Swinging his lantern, the captain paced back and forth on the beach, while the wind howled and the waves crashed. Then, in the light of a lightning flash, he saw something swimming towards him. It was Molly. There was someone clinging to her, clutching her thick fur.

Back inside the warm lighthouse, the rescued fisherman huddled by the fire, wrapped in blankets. As he sipped his hot almost-instant seaweed soup, he marvelled over his rescue.

"That's what Newfies do," said the captain, proudly.

Molly became known as the Lighthouse Dog, and only once did she ever go back to town. That was the day she received her shiny, almost-silver lifesaving medal from the captain's wife's friend Flossie's uncle on her father's side, the mayor.

To the Victoria Hospice, the P. R.T. and Marilyn

B.W.

For Sonja the Fair, Queen of the Back Scratchers
and Anna, Carmen and Mimi for most
conspicuous piggery.

D.G.

Text copyright © 1997 Betty Waterton
Illustration copyright © 1997 Dean Griffiths

Orca Book Publishers gratefully acknowledges the support for our publishing
programs provided by the following agencies: the Department of Canadian
Heritage, the Canada Council for the Arts, and the British Columbia Ministry of
Small Business, Tourism and Culture.

Orca Book Publishers
PO Box 5626, Station B
Victoria, BC V8R 6S4
Canada

Orca Book Publishers
PO Box 468
Custer, WA 98240-0468
USA

Canadian Cataloguing in Publication Data
Waterton, Betty, 1923 –
The lighthouse dog

ISBN 1-55143-073-8 (bound)
1. Newfoundland dog — juvenile fiction. I. Griffiths, Dean, 1967 –
II. Title.
PS8595.A796L53 1997   jC813'.54   C97–910430–0
PZ7.W2644Li 1997

Library of Congress Catalog Card Number: 97-67366

Design by Christine Toller
Printed and bound in Hong Kong

99 98 97   5 4 3 2 1

199